Where's Al?

Byron Barton

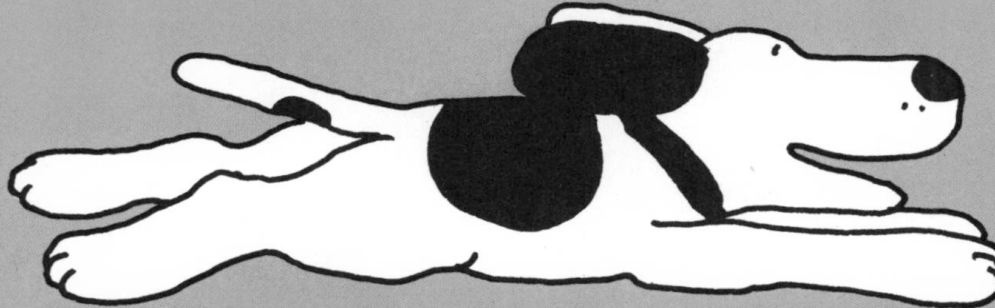

Houghton Mifflin/Clarion Books/New York

L.C. Catalog Card Number: 78-171866.
ISBN: 0-395-28765-0
(Previously published by the Seabury Press under ISBN: 0-8164-3088-8)
Third Printing

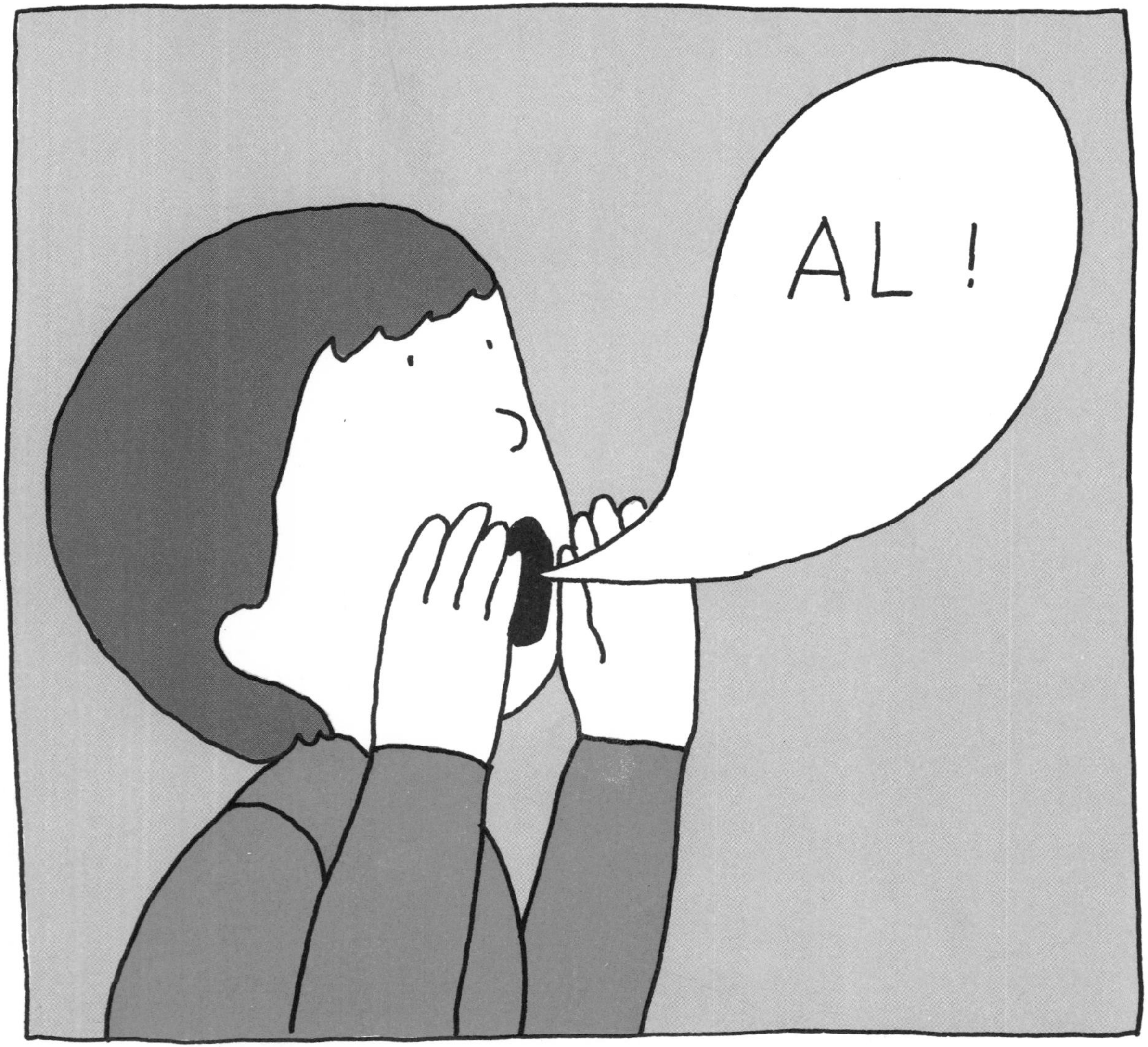
AL!

Where's Al?

Al is lost.

I'm not hungry.

I can't sleep.

I'll find Al today.

sanitation

LOST DOG
REWARD

Did you find a dog?

Lost
dog
reward
200 3rd av

I Lost my dog.

hot dogs

Sanitation

Fruits
Veget

hot dogs
Did you see a dog?

Fruits

hot dogs
sanitation

Ruff !

hot dogs
Sanitation

Fruits
AL!

CDEFGHIJ—RA—8765432 /80

12345

Barton, Byron

Where's Al?